THIS BOOK BELONGS TO:

Celebrate Kipper's 18th birthday
with other Kipper books:

Kipper
Kipper's Toybox
Kipper's Birthday
Kipper's Monster
Kipper and Roly
Kipper's Beach Ball

Storyboards:

Butterfly	Castle
Hisssss!	Miaow!
Honk!	Playtime!
Splosh!	Swing!

Visit www.hodderchildrens.co.uk/Kipper
for fun and games

Skates

Mick Inkpen

Hodder
Children's
Books

A division of Hachette Children's Books

Tiger had some brand new skates.

'They're called Roller Blades,' said Tiger. 'Much better than ordinary skates, Kipper. Look, the wheels are all in a line!'

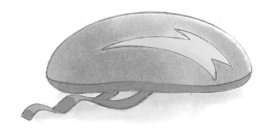

Tiger was not very good on his new skates. He kept wobbling and falling on his bottom.

Then he rolled off down the path, waving his arms and shouting, 'Get out of the way!'

He crashed into Pig, who was walking Arnold in the park.

Tiger struggled to his feet, and then fell over again.

'I haven't got any skates,' said Pig. 'Can I have a go?'

'Ow!' shouted Tiger.
He had hurt his thumb.
'Ow! Ow! Ow!' He wasn't
very brave.

Kipper took him home for
a sticking plaster. Tiger wanted
some ointment, a bandage,
a sling and a sweetie too!

'Let's go and show Pig my
bandage!' he said.

When they arrived at
Pig's house, Pig and
Arnold were in the garden.
Pig was still wearing
Kipper's skates.

'I want to show you
something!' said Pig. He put
on some music and began
to skate.

'What you need is practice,' said Tiger. He was so busy telling Pig how to do it, that he didn't notice himself rolling down the slope again.

He crashed into a bush.

'No,' said Tiger.
'No, I wouldn't want
you to hurt yourself. No.'

So Kipper let Pig have a
go of his skates instead.

Pig was a terrible skater.
He couldn't even stand up!

'Wow!' said Kipper and Tiger together.
Pig had been practising.
He was brilliant!

And Arnold wasn't bad, either.

First published in 2001 by Hodder Children's Books
A division of Hachette Children's Books, 338 Euston Road, London, NW1 3BH

Hachette Children's Books Australia, Level 17/207 Kent Street, Sydney, NSW 2000

Copyright © Mick Inkpen 2001
Illustrations © Hodder Children's Books 2001

The right of Mick Inkpen to be identified as the author
and the illustrator of this Work has been asserted by him in
accordance with the Copyright, Designs and Patents Act 1988.

Illustrations by Stuart Trotter

A catalogue record of this book is available from the British Library.

ISBN: 978 0 340 81814 5
10 9 8 7 6 5 4 3 2

Printed in China

Hodder Children's Books is a division of Hachette Children's Books
An Hachette Livre UK Company